DULUTH PUBLIC LIBRARY

WITHDRAWN

Healthy Eating Choices

BY MEGAN BAILEY

Published by The Child's World®
1980 Lookout Drive • Mankato, MN 56003-1705
800-599-READ • www.childsworld.com

Acknowledgments
The Child's World®: Mary Berendes, Publishing Director
Red Line Editorial: Editorial direction
The Design Lab: Design
Amnet: Production
Photographs ©: Front cover: Creativa/Shutterstock Images; FoodIcons; BrandX Images; FoodIcons, 2, 3, 8, 9, 12, 14; BrandX Images, 4, 6, 10, 15, 19, 21 (top-right and top-left); glenda/Shutterstock Images, 5; choosemyplate.gov, 7; Monkey Business Images/Shutterstock Images, 11; ElenaGaak/Shutterstock Images, 13; kurhan/Shutterstock Images, 16; Shelby Allison/Shutterstock Images, 17; mexrix/Shutterstock Images, 18; marco mayer/Shutterstock Images, 21 (bottom)

Copyright © 2014 by The Child's World®
All rights reserved. No part of this book may be reproduced or utilized in any form or by any means without written permission from the publisher.

ISBN: 978-1623235406
LCCN: 2013931337

Printed in the United States of America
Mankato, MN
July, 2013
PA02174

ABOUT THE AUTHOR
Megan Bailey is a freelance writer who works from her home in Chicago. She loves kids, pets, especially cats, and the Chicago Cubs.

Table of Contents

CHAPTER 1	A Healthy Plate	**4**
CHAPTER 2	Food Facts	**10**
CHAPTER 3	Reading Food Labels	**16**

Hands-on Activity:
   Healthy Cooking Challenge — **20**
Glossary — **22**
To Learn More — **23**
Index — **24**

CHAPTER ONE

A Healthy Plate

▶ *Opposite page: Pizza can be healthy if you use nutritious ingredients such as vegetables and whole-grain dough.*

Allison went over to her friend Chelsea's house after school one day to play. She was excited when Chelsea's mother invited her to stay for dinner. To Allison's surprise, Chelsea's mom wanted Chelsea and Allison to help make dinner that night. The only thing Allison had ever cooked was toast! Chelsea's mom said that it was okay. They would teach her about cooking.

Helping make dinner sounded a little less scary when Allison found out that they would be making pizza. Pizza was Allison's favorite food. Chelsea's mom had picked up a whole-wheat pizza crust from the store. She said that whole-wheat pizza crust was a healthier choice than regular crust. They

▲ *Mushrooms are healthy toppings for your pizza.*

spread the pizza sauce on the crust and sprinkled on the cheese. Then, Chelsea's mom brought out the toppings. Allison was surprised to see broccoli, mushrooms, and spinach! Chelsea could tell Allison was surprised. She explained that vegetables are delicious and healthy pizza toppings.

The pizza looked pretty tasty when it came out of the oven. Allison liked all the different colors the vegetables added to the pizza. When Allison took a bite, there were so many flavors in her mouth. She really liked the pizza, even better than her usual pepperoni slice!

When she helped Chelsea and her mom cook dinner, Allison learned more about healthy eating choices. By including vegetables and **whole grains**, she was eating a well-balanced meal. She learned that choosing healthy ingredients could taste great, too.

▶ *Opposite page: The MyPlate guidelines show you how to balance your meals for healthy eating.*

▲ *Broccoli is another good-for-you topping for your pizza.*

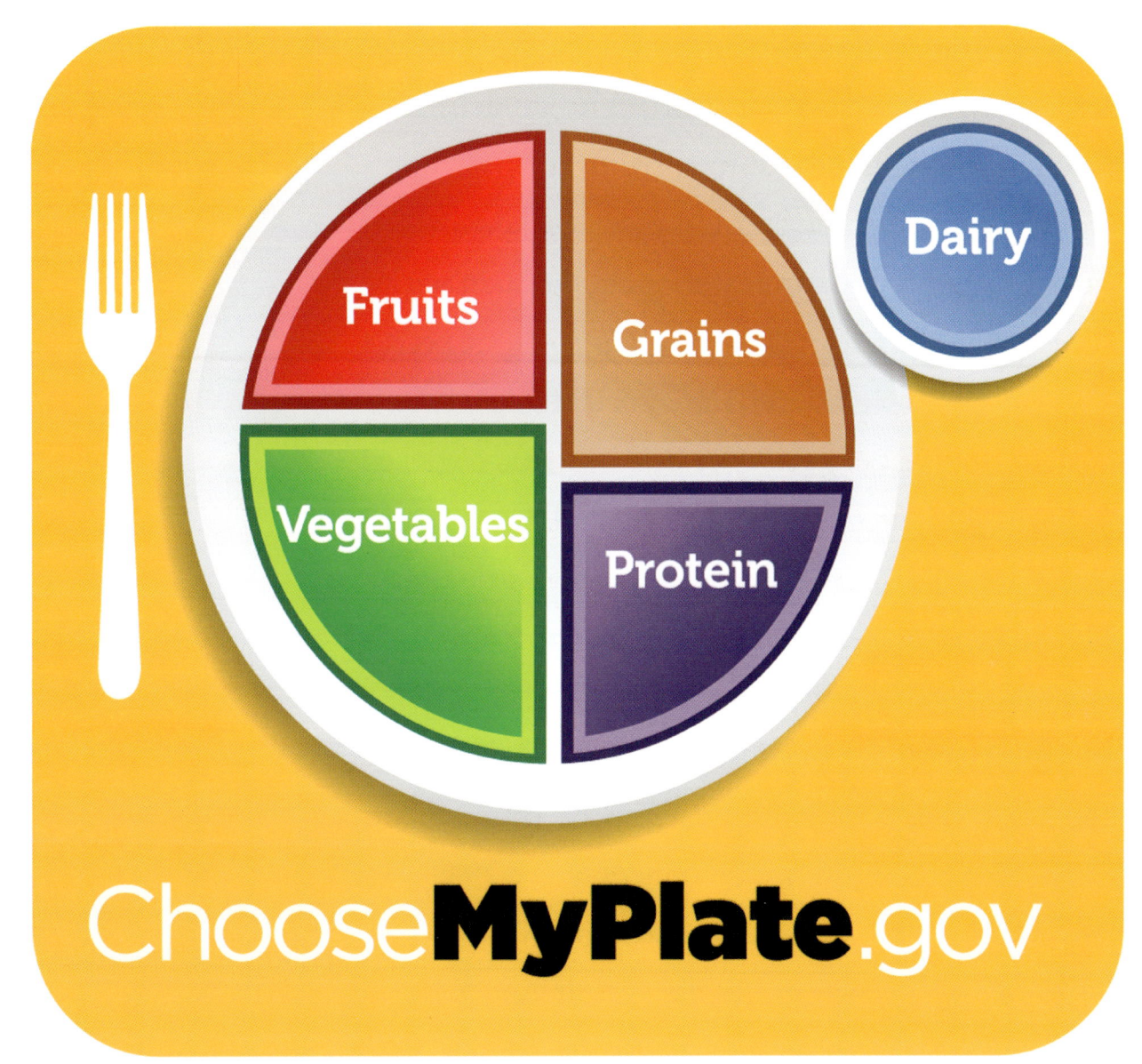

It is easy to make healthy eating choices like Allison and Chelsea did. The MyPlate guidelines show that you need to eat foods from the five major food groups: fruits, vegetables, **protein**, grains, and dairy. Half of your plate should be filled with fruits and vegetables. Kids ages four to eight need 1 to 1 1/2 cups of fruits and 1 1/2 cups of vegetables every day. Kids between nine and 13 years old need 1 1/2 cups of fruits every day. Girls ages nine to 13 need 2 cups of vegetables every day, while boys ages nine to 13 need 2 1/2 cups each day.

Protein foods include meat, eggs, beans, nuts, seeds, and soy. Kids ages four to eight need 4 ounces of protein every day. Kids between nine and 13 years old need 5 ounces of protein each day. Most people have plenty of protein in their diets already. But, it may not always be healthy protein. Healthy

OUTSTANDING OILS

Oils are another part of a balanced diet, but they are not considered their own food group. Oils are found in different plants and fish. They provide important nutrients for your body. Most people get enough oil in their diets from foods that contain oils, such as nuts and fish.

▼ *Stir-fry can include healthy vegetables and protein foods.*

▲ *Grain foods such as these whole-grain rolls are part of the MyPlate guidelines.*

protein choices include lean meats and beans.

Grains and dairy are the last two food groups. Grain foods are essential parts of a healthy diet. Grain foods include bread, rice, oatmeal, and popcorn. Kids ages four to eight and girls ages nine to 13 should eat 5 ounces of grains every day. Boys nine to 13 years old should eat 6 ounces of grains every day. About half of these ounces should be whole grains. Whole grains are made from the entire grain seed. They include foods such as brown rice, oatmeal, and whole-wheat flour. The dairy group includes milk and foods made from milk. The amount of dairy a person needs in his or her diet usually depends on his or her age. The average healthy amount of dairy for children is 2 1/2 to 3 cups each day.

CHAPTER TWO

Food Facts

Eating a balanced diet is an important part of keeping your body healthy. Each food group has important nutrients and **vitamins** that help your body grow and stay strong. **Carbohydrates**, protein, **fats**, vitamins, and **minerals** all help your body grow strong and healthy.

Some of the most important nutrients found in food are carbohydrates. Carbohydrates are in each of the five food groups. Your body breaks down carbohydrates into sugars to use as energy. There are two types of carbohydrates. Simple carbohydrates are the sugars found in foods such as fruit and milk. Complex carbohydrates are carbohydrates the body has to break down into sugars before it can use the

▶ *Opposite page: Eating a balanced lunch with vegetables, fruit, and protein helps you get all the nutrients you need.*

▲ *Raspberries and other fruits contain carbohydrates.*

carbohydrates as energy. Whole-grain breads and cereals contain complex carbohydrates.

Protein is not just a food group. It is also an essential nutrient. Your body uses protein to repair and replace parts such as organs and **tissues**. It even uses protein to keep your blood healthy. Protein is especially important for a healthy body and mind while you are growing up. You can get protein from eating foods such as lean meat, fish, poultry, beans, and nuts.

Fats are another important part of a healthy diet. Fat is usually thought of as a bad thing. Eating too much of the wrong kinds of fats can lead to health problems and **obesity**. However, you still need fats in your diet because they give your body energy and help your body grow as you get older. Fats are also needed to absorb vitamins from food. Get fats from healthy foods such as olive oil, nuts, and fish.

▶ *Opposite page: Fish such as this grilled salmon is a good source of healthy fats.*

▼ *Beef kabobs provide protein from the lean meat and vitamins and minerals from the vegetables.*

Making healthy food choices means you are getting a healthy amount of vitamins and minerals from the foods you eat. Vitamins and minerals keep you healthy, growing, and strong. There are many different kinds of vitamins that play special roles in keeping your body healthy. For example, vitamin C, which is found in many fruits and vegetables, helps your body fight off illness. Minerals such as **calcium** are needed to build strong bones and teeth. Calcium also helps your heart and muscles work properly. Find vitamins and minerals in healthy foods such as dairy foods, nuts, and lots of fruits and vegetables.

DUMP THE JUNK FOOD
Not all food is created equally. Junk food, such as fast food and sugary drinks, are not healthy for your body. Junk food does not contain the proper amount of nutrients your body needs to stay healthy. This type of food can have too much fat and sugar. Eating too much junk food can cause health problems, obesity, and a bad body image.

◄ *Nuts are a great source of protein and healthy fats.*

► *Opposite page: Making wise eating choices helps your body and mind grow strong and healthy.*

CHAPTER THREE

Reading Food Labels

▼ *Nutrition Facts Labels help you make healthy choices at the grocery store.*

It is not easy to know if a food is healthy just by looking at it. However, a little detective work can help you figure out if the food you are going to eat is healthy. Many foods have a black-and-white box printed on their packaging called the **Nutrition Facts Label**.

The Nutrition Facts Label is a food's report card. It tells you what kinds of nutrients are in a food. It lists the amount of **calories**,

Nutrition Facts	
Serving Size 5 oz. (144g)	
Servings Per Container 4	

Amount Per Serving	
Calories 310	**Calories** from Fat 100

	% Daily Value*
Total Fat 15g	21%
Saturated Fat 2.6g	17%
Trans Fat 1g	
Cholesterol 118mg	39%
Sodium 560mg	28%
Total Carbohydrate 12g	4%
Dietary Fiber 1g	4%
Sugars 1g	
Protein 24g	

Vitamin A 1%	•	Vitamin C 2%
Calcium 2%	•	**Iron** 5%

*Percent Daily Values are based on a 2,000 calorie diet. Your daily values may be higher or lower depending on your calorie needs:

	Calories	2,000	2,500
Total Fat	Less Than	65g	80g
Saturated Fat	Less Than	20g	25g
Cholesterol	Less Than	300mg	300mg
Sodium	Less Than	2,400mg	2,400mg
Total Carbohydrate		300g	375g
Dietary Fiber		25g	30g

Calories per gram:
 Fat 9 • Carbohydrate 4 • Protein 4

▲ *Read the Nutrition Facts Label to know how many calories and nutrients are in a food.*

carbohydrates, protein, fats, vitamins, and minerals that are in a serving. You can also use the Nutrition Facts Label to compare different foods. Imagine you have two different types of bread in your cupboard. You can use the Nutrition Facts Labels on the breads to figure out which one is healthier. Look to see which bread has more vitamins or less sugar.

Your family can use Nutrition Facts Labels to purchase healthy foods at the grocery store. Then, you can use these healthy ingredients to cook up healthy snacks and meals. Here are a few ideas:

- Use ground turkey instead of ground beef to make burgers.
- Choose whole-grain pasta instead of regular pasta for your spaghetti.
- Slurp soups made with vegetable broth instead of cream.

- Choose low-fat cottage cheese and yogurt instead of full-fat options.
- Use brown rice or wild rice instead of white rice for your stir-fry.

Nutrition Facts Labels are put on food packaging to help you make healthier food choices. They help teach you about the food you eat. Reading these labels is an easy way to make sure you are making healthy eating choices.

SERVING SIZES
Another tip when reading the Nutrition Facts Labels is to check out the recommended serving size. This is usually one of the first things listed on the label. It tells you how much one serving of a food item is, such as one slice of bread. If you are eating more than the recommended serving size, then the nutrition facts for your serving go up. That means, if you are eating two slices of bread, the amount of nutrients will be doubled, too.

◄ *Choose low-fat yogurt and add fruit or granola for a healthy snack.*

► *Opposite page: Use a food's ingredient list to make healthy eating choices.*

Hands-on Activity: Healthy Cooking Challenge

Your healthy cooking challenge is to make a healthy, delicious pizza!

What You'll Need:

Whole-wheat pizza crust, tomato sauce, low-fat shredded cheese, vegetables for toppings

Directions:

Have your parent or another adult go with you to the grocery store to find your pizza ingredients. Remember to make healthy choices by picking ingredients that are in the healthy food groups. Once you have your ingredients, follow these steps to make a healthy, delicious pizza:

1. Have an adult help you chop your vegetables.
2. Roll out your dough.
3. Spread your sauce and sprinkle your cheese.
4. Top off the pizza with your vegetables.
5. Bake and enjoy!

Glossary

calcium (KAL-see-um): Calcium is an essential nutrient. Calcium helps build strong bones and teeth.

calories (KAL-ur-eez): Calories are measurements of energy that your body gets from food. Kids need calories to play sports and to do well in school.

carbohydrates (kar-bo-HY-drayts): Carbohydrates are parts of food that provide energy for the body. There are simple and complex carbohydrates.

fats (fats): Fats are parts of food that provide energy for the body. Fats help the body use some of the vitamins found in food.

minerals (MIN-er-ulz): Minerals are elements found in foods and needed for the body to function. People can get many of their daily minerals from fruits and vegetables.

nutrients (NOO-tree-ents): Nutrients are substances the body needs to grow. Vitamins and minerals are nutrients.

Nutrition Facts Label (noo-TRI-shun faks LAY-bul): The Nutrition Facts Label is a part of food packaging that tells what kinds of nutrients are in a food and how many nutrients a food has. Use the Nutrition Facts Label to discover if a food is healthy.

obesity (oh-BEES-it-ee): Obesity occurs when a person weighs much more than what is healthy for his or her body. Eating too many calories and not being physically active may lead to obesity.

protein (PRO-teen): Protein is a part of food that provides energy for your body and contains nutrients used by the whole body. Protein is found in meat, nuts, and seeds.

tissues (TISH-yooz): Tissues are made up of groups of cells that do the same thing in your body. Your body uses protein to rebuild tissues.

vitamins (VYE-tuh-minz): Vitamins are substances found in foods and help our bodies function properly. Fruits and vegetables are good sources of vitamins.

whole grains (hol GRAYNZ): Whole grains contain all the nutrients of a grain seed. Fiber, minerals, and vitamins are found in whole grains.

To Learn More

BOOKS

Miller, Edward. *The Monster Health Book: A Guide to Eating Healthy, Being Active & Feeling Great for Monsters & Kids!* New York: Holiday House, 2006.

Zinczenko, David and Matt Goulding. *Eat This Not That! For Kids! Be the Leanest, Fittest Family on the Block!* Emmaus, PA: Rodale, 2008.

WEB SITES

Visit our Web site for links about making healthy eating choices: **childsworld.com/links**

Note to Parents, Teachers, and Librarians: We routinely verify our Web links to make sure they are safe and active sites. So encourage your readers to check them out!

Index

calories, 17, 22
carbohydrates, 10–12, 17, 22

dairy foods, 14
    cottage cheese, 18
    cream, 17
    milk, 9, 10
    yogurt, 18

fats, 10, 12, 14, 17, 18, 22
    fish, 8, 12
    nuts, 8, 12, 14
    oils, 8, 12
food groups, 7, 8, 9, 10, 12, 20
    dairy, 7, 8, 9
    fruits, 7, 8
    grains, 7, 8, 9
    protein, 7, 8–9
    vegetables, 7, 8
fruits, 8, 10, 14, 18, 22
    raspberries, 10

grain foods, 4, 6, 9, 12, 17
    bread, 9, 12, 17, 18
    flour, 9
    granola, 18
    oatmeal, 9
    pasta, 17
    popcorn, 9
    rice, 9, 18

healthy cooking challenge, 20

junk food, 14

minerals, 10, 12, 14, 17, 22
    calcium, 14, 22
MyPlate, 6, 7, 8, 9

nutrients, 8, 10, 12, 14, 16, 17, 18, 22
Nutrition Facts Label, 16–18, 22

obesity, 12, 14, 22

pizza, 4–6, 20
protein foods, 8–9, 10, 12, 14, 17
    beans, 8, 9, 12
    eggs, 8
    fish, 8, 12
    meat, 8, 9, 12, 22
    nuts, 8, 12, 14, 22
    poultry, 12, 17
    seeds, 8, 22
    soy, 8

serving sizes, 8–9, 17, 18
stir-fry, 8, 18

vegetables, 4, 6, 8, 10, 12, 14, 17, 20, 22
    broccoli, 6
    mushrooms, 4, 6
    spinach, 6
vitamins, 10, 12, 14, 17, 22
    vitamin C, 14

whole grains, 4, 6, 9, 12, 17, 20, 22